THE HAMMER C
VIBERT MII

This book is a work of fiction. All names, characters and incidents are products of the author's imagination. Any resemblance to persons, living or dead, is purely coincidental.

Copyright @ 2024 by Vibert Miller

All rights reserved

Cover design by V. A. Miller

CHAPTER 1

Jack Peregrin was not one to be indecisive as to what path he should take. He was a man who examined a problem from all angles and made up his mind as to how he should proceed. Yet, here he was awash in indecision and in the throes of ambivalence.

Abby was standing behind him massaging the tight muscles in his shoulders. "This is not you" she said. "You're as tense as a long-tailed cat in a room full of rocking chairs."

"A long-tailed cat?" he said, "I've noticed the homespun tidbits that have crept into your language recently."

"You don't like it," she said.

"It's not that I don't like it," he said, "It's just unusual coming from you."

"I'm mentoring a new recruit fresh out of the Academy, He's from a small town in Alabama and he's brought his southern homespun tidbits, as you call them, with him. I think some of them are cute."

"So, I can expect to hear more," Jack said.

"Well, I can be more aware of what I say around you," Abby said.

"Please, Abby," Jack said, "don't do that. We've always spoken freely to each other. I don't want that to change. I may find some of those southern sayings appealing and start using them myself. Promise me you will not adjust how you speak to me. I might even learn something from your recruit."

"You still haven't told me what's bothering you so much," Abby said. "Oh. I know. You've met another woman and you can't decide which one of us you want." Abby was smiling as she said this.

"That would be easy," Jack said, "you'd win hands down. No. I have to make a decision that would have far reaching consequences for both of us."

"Oh, oh. This sounds serious," Abby said easing down into the chair next to the one Jack was sitting in.

He stared ahead for a few seconds and then looked her in the eye. "I heard from Tom Cummings," he said in a small voice.

"Tom Cummings?" Abby said, "who is Tom...?" she stopped and bolted out of her chair. "WHAT? WHAT?"

"He was contacted by someone high up in the government. They want him to revive the agency and..."

"WHAT? What does that have to do with you, Jack?" Abby said.

"He was making calls to see if he could bring back the old team. I was among those he called."

"And you said?"

"I said I would think about it."

"You would think about it? Not, 'no Tom.' I would think about it." Abby was livid. Her beautiful, serene face had transformed into a dark storm cloud.

"Well Jack Peregrin," she said, "add this to your thoughts. If you leave to go off fighting bad guys around the globe, I, too, am leaving. I will not go through that living hell again."

"I know," Jack said quietly and watched Abby disappear up the stairs.

In his former life, Jack Peregrin, was a mercenary with an outfit known only as The Agency. It was a quasi-government organization set up to combat crime across the globe by doing things no government can be seen doing. It gave deniability. It was very effective but to do their jobs the agents had to disappear when they were in the field. This drove Abby into the pits of grief. She never knew where in the world Jack was or if he was alive or dead. The name Thomas Cummings had come to mean a living hell to Abby. Tom was the head of the organization and the one who sent out the agents. The day they disbanded was the happiest day of her life. Now, Tom was back threatening to take away everything that meant life to her. This time would be different. She had no control over what Jack or Tom did but she had control over her own life.

"Thinking about, he said," she thought. "Well, I, too, will think about it."

Jack remained seated and had his eyes fixed on the stairs Abby just ascended. He heard the bedroom door close. He never believed the nonsense, he thought, of his ancestor, a Lakota Sioux warrior could speak to him but he would welcome such an intervention right now.

Abby was a trooper with the Maryland Highway Patrol out of Bethesda. She met Jack when she pulled him over for speeding a few years back. She saved his life then because his heart was about to give out. On a mission in Peru, he had run afoul of some drug traffickers whose aim was to kill him but he survived with a damaged heart. His body was trying to refuse the new heart and that was the reason he was speeding to the hospital when Abby intervened and eventually fell in love with him. Her life then was one of constant despair because each time he left to go on a mission she was never sure she would see him alive again or if she would see him at all. After The Agency broke up and she had her man back, she made a silent vow she would never put herself through that hell again. But that hell was threatening to return. Abby had a momentous decision to make and she knew she did not have the fortitude to make it.

Jack went up the stairs to the bedroom he shared with Abby. For a brief moment he expected to find the door locked but it wasn't. He went in and found Abby sitting by a window that gave unto the lake. She was staring at some ducks that were paddling about on the smooth surface. He hesitated but went up to her and placed a hand on her shoulder. She stiffened but did not brush his hand off. Neither one spoke until Abby broke the silence.

"I have a decision to make, also," she said.

"I know," Jack said. "but please wait. I have not made mine."

"It doesn't matter," she said, "the fact that you did not immediately say no to Mr. Cummings, speaks volumes."

"Yes," he said. "I realize that. To make it less uncomfortable for both of us, I will move into one of the guest bedrooms."

"No," she said, "I will. This is your house after all."

Jack winced at that. This was the first time Abby had referred to the house as his.

She immediately walked over to the big walk-in closet and started to remove her clothes. Jack stood by helpless as the woman he loved began the process of removing herself from his life.

Two days later, when Abby did not return home from work at the time she did usually, an emptiness flooded him. He ran upstairs to the bedroom she was occupying. The bed was made and the room felt empty. He opened the clothes closet and it was empty. Abby was gone. Just to be sure he checked the other guest bedroom and his own master bedroom. There was no sign of Abby. It would not have been good for a big, tough detective to cry but he wanted to.

CHAPTER 2

A week after Abby left, Jack was in his office at his desk when the door swung open and Abby's sister walked in.

"Hello Margaret, " Jack said.

"Don't hello Margaret, me," she said, "if I were taller I'd punch you in the nose."

"And my nose might welcome it," Jack said. "How is she?"

"If by she you mean Abby, she's fine. She's holed up in my guest room but fine. And for some reason beyond my understanding, she misses you."

"I miss her too," Jack said.

"And that's why you're thinking of going out to roam the world and probably get yourself killed." Margaret retorted.

"That has not been decided," Jack said, "I don't have a death wish."

"Ha. Fine talk," Margaret said, "Just the idea you're considering it is enough to drive any woman away. Even a strong woman like my sister. Okay, I've had my say. I'll leave you with your thoughts. And for the record, Abby doesn't know I'm here." Margaret walked purposefully to the door, stood in front of it as if trying to remember something more she wanted to say. It didn't come to her so she shook her head in resignation, opened the door and went out

"How are the girls?" Jack called out. She just raised her hand and kept on walking. The girls he was asking about were Margaret's two small daughters.

"I guess they're fine," he muttered to himself.

His cell phone buzzed and ID showed it was Tom Cummings. He answered it and before Cummings could say anything Jack started in.

"Sorry, Tom," he said, "I can't do it. I can't uproot my life and become a mercenary again."

"Hello Jack," Cummings said. "You always were one to jump the gun. I'm calling to tell you we're not reviving The Agency. Funding fell through. But I'm thinking Abby had something to do with your decision."

"Yeah," he said, "but she left me."

"Sorry to hear that buddy. I hope this news will bring her back. By the way, I was not entirely committed to the idea. If it comes up again I will say no at the outset."

> "Where are you, Tom? I would like to see you," Jack said
> "You'll have to cross the pond, Lad, I'm still in Scotland.:
> "Well, Erin Go Bragh to you, Tom," Jack said
> "And to you, Slainte," Tom replied and disconnected..
> After Tom was gone, Jack punched the air with his fist and shouted, "Yes."

The decision was taken from him and it felt as if someone had removed the weight of the world from his shoulders. He was Atlas heaving the globe away from him.

Jack was stunned when his office door opened and Abby walked into his office. He stood and stared at her not trusting himself to say anything. She approached and hugged him.

"Am I dreaming?" he said, "or is it really Abby?"

"No, Jack," she said, "you're not dreaming. It is me, in the flesh. How are you?"

"I'm fine, Abby," he responded, "and you?"

"I have been better," she said. "I miss you."

"That goes double for me," Jack said.

"And that brings me to why I'm here," she said..

"Before you say anything else," he said, "I want you to know The Agency is not coming back. Tom told me."

"Oh?"

"Yes. But before he told me that, I told him I was not interested. I had no intention of leaving my life with you. But more importantly I didn't want to put you through that hell, again."

Abby stared at him. "Jack Peregrin," she said, "you don't fight fair. I came here prepared to convince you not to go back into the field and expose yourself to danger. But you just took all the wind out of my sails."

"Does that mean you're moving back in with me?" Jack said.

"It does on one condition. You let me occupy one of the guest rooms for a bit. Just until I've convinced myself I'm doing the right thing."

"Condition accepted," Jack said. "I'm happy to have you near me, even in a room down the hall. I have a feeling you're seeing this as a trial run and you're not as fully committed as you were."

"Maybe," she said, "I'll move my things in tonight."

She stood, gave him her cheek to kiss and left.

Jack stared after her, feeling euphoria seep into his gut. His Abby was coming home. His world was back on its axis and spinning merrily along. Until the door opened and Margaret and her daughters breezed in. The girls immediately ran to him and circled their arms around him. Jack raised his hand as his ancestors did. "How," he said.

"Never mind that," Margaret said, "my sister told me she was moving back in with you. That's well and good. Just watch yourself, buster. I've been told we're descended from Vikings. And you know the reputation they had."

She turned to leave, herding her daughters out with a "come along girls."

Both of the young ones giggled, "yeah, watch yourself, Uncle Jack."

"Vikings?" Jack said to the empty office, "Abby never told me that."

CHAPTER 3

Abby said goodnight to Jack and headed up the stairs to the guest bedroom she was using. She entered and got a very strange feeling. The room looked as if no one lived in it and that was confirmed when she opened the closet to retrieve her nightgown. It was empty. All her clothes were gone. She went to the other guest bedroom thinking she had the wrong room. But that too was empty. Jack was still in the living room watching a show.

"Were we robbed?" she asked.

"Robbed? Why do you think that?" Jack said.

"All my clothes are gone," she replied.

"Oh, that," Jack said, "have you looked in the master bedroom?"

"I have not. That's where you live. Why would my clothes be in your closet?"

"Maybe because I put them there," Jack said.

"That implies I would be sleeping in your bed," Abby said. "Is that your intention, Mister?"

"I was hoping," Jack said. "I don't even remember what came between us."

"You mean, bury the hatchet," Abby said.

"Yeah,. As long as you're not eyeing my back."

Jack went into the dining room and retrieved a bottle of bourbon from a cabinet and glasses and ice from the kitchen, then sat next to Abby on the sofa. They clinked glasses.

"What are we toasting to?" she asked.

"To a renewed relationship," he said raising his glass. She also raised her glass.

Jack placed his glass on the coffee table, took her glass from her hand and placed it beside his. Then he pulled her in and tried to find her lips. But she moved her head to one side and pushed him back. She got up and walked over to another chair.

"Moving my clothes to your closet does not solve anything," she said.

"I agree," he said, "I just thought it was a way to begin the process of melting the iceberg that has moved in between us."

"Mmm."

"Can you use words?"

"Yes. Let's talk tomorrow. Right now, it's bedtime for me."

"May I lead you to bed?" Jack said offering his hand to her.

"You may," she replied taking it.

They were in bed stretched out on their sides.

"I've just realized something," Jack said.

"What's that?"

"This bed is too large."

She started to remind him it was his idea to get a large bed but instead, she said, "We could meet halfway," and shifted to the center. Jack met her and tentatively put an arm around her. She responded and sought his lips. Then she rolled on top of him so their bodies were touching in all the erotic places. The kiss was deep and long and caused both of them to feel the electricity coursing through their veins.

"I love you dearly, Abby," he said, "and I've missed you."

"Mmm," she said as he reached under her nightgown and caressed her.

Afterwards Abby said, "I think we've melted your iceberg."

"It wasn't *my* iceberg. But yes, we've melted it."

Abby was quiet for a long time and Jack became apprehensive. He wondered if the problem had come back.

"Why so quiet?" he asked her.

"I was trying to remember what drove us apart. I don't remember. Do you?"

"Honestly, no," he said.

"It's a little bit like the Hatfields and the McCoys," Abby said, "after so many generations of shooting at each other they forgot what the fight was about in the first place."

Abby nestled in Jack's arms and in a short while he could hear her gentle breathing. Then he. too, slipped into sleep.

Abby was still asleep when Jack awoke so he quietly went into the bathroom to get dressed and slipped down to the kitchen to make breakfast. He was putting the food on the table when she came down. She was still in her nightgown but her hair was done up and she had spent time making herself even more beautiful than she was. A huge smile covered Jack's face when he saw her. He ran over and pulled out a chair for her.

"Wow," she said, "if this is the treatment I get after an argument, I'm tempted to argue more. Did your ancestors treat their women this way?"

"I don't know," Jack said, "but I can answer your question with an old joke I heard someplace. A chief was riding his horse with his woman walking beside him. Someone shouted out to him, 'how come you're riding and your woman's walking?' to which the chief replied, 'woman walk 'cause she don't got no hoss.'"

Jack brought a small jug to the table and poured two glasses for them. "You made mimosas?" Abby said.

"Yes," he replied, "to celebrate our new relationship."

She stood and wrapped herself around him. "I'll never get tired of hearing you tell me you love me," she said, "and I'll never tire of telling you I do."

"Okay," he said, "let's enjoy this delicious breakfast."

"And when we're done I want you to take me upstairs and help me out of my nightgown."

"That's a duty I will take great pleasure in performing," Jack said and his broad smile showed he meant it.

Jack and Abby never spoke again of the reason for their temporary split. It was as if they had put that behind them and wanted to leave it there.

Abby was getting dressed and Jack was watching her.

"Is there a reason I have your undivided attention?" She asked.

"Yes, there is," he answered. "I was wondering what I had done to merit the love of such a beautiful woman."

She stopped and stared at him. "Alright. What are you aiming at? And just so you know, your chances of getting whatever it is you want are very good."

"You make me want to go out and leap tall buildings," Jack said.

"I thought that is what you do," Abby said. "Am I wrong?"

"The only leaping I'm going to do right now is to jump over to where you are and kiss you until you beg for mercy."

"Okay, big guy," she said, "show me."

Margaret and her girls stopped by that afternoon and the girls immediately surrounded Jack.

"My husband is mad at you|" Margaret said to Jack.. "He thinks his daughters think more of you than they do of him."

"Can you blame them?" Jack said.

"Abby," Margaret said, "where did you find this man?"

"Well, I pulled him over for speeding and..."

"I already know the story," Margaret said with her hinds up to stop Abby. "And you, Chief Peregrin, what kind of name is that?"

"Mom," the older girl spoke up, "the Peregrin Falcon is a bird of prey. It hunts by swooping down very fast on other birds."

Margaret was staring at her daughter then she turned to Jack, "did you teach her that?"

"Me? No way."

"Mom," her daughter said, "we had a lesson on birds of prey in school." She turned to Jack and asked him, "is that why your name is Peregrin?"

"Well, Chief?" Margaret said. "Seems, to me, it's time for a history lesson."

Jack looked at Abby for help but she just smiled at him and said, "don't look at me. I'm not descended from a fierce warrior who wanted to name himself after a raptor but couldn't spell and left off the final *e* from his name."

"You've wrapped up my ancestry in one beautiful sentence," Jack said, "thank you."

CHAPTER 4

After Margaret and her daughters left, Abby told Jack she was working the graveyard shift that night.

"For the next five days?" Jack said.

"No," she replied, "just tonight. Captain called and asked if I could stand in for another trooper who is sick."

She had just parked in her favorite place along the highway and settled down to watch for speeders, when she saw high beams coming at her. The driver was running all out in the wrong lane. The car passed her and she saw it was a woman and it reminded Abby of a private saying among troopers. The woman was driving with her pedal nailed to the floor. Abby called it in to dispatch who told her not to give chase. They were aware of the speeder and had a road block set up further down the highway.

"At her speed, a roadblock will kill her," Abby said.

"We are aware of that," the dispatcher said, "but she's driving at high speed heading East in a West bound lane. She's putting a lot of people at risk."

This was only the second time Abby had encountered this in all her years as a patrol officer. She knew, instinctively, this would result in the same way. This driver was heading into a major crash that would kill her and probably many other people.

But Abby was wrong. A few minutes later her radio came alive. It was dispatch telling her, the speeding car had crossed the median and was now running West. Abby would soon see the car and it was her call whether or not to pursue. The car flashed by. Abby called dispatch to let them know and asked why the driver was in such a hurry.

"She's on the run," dispatch said. The woman and two others had broken out of prison. They were cornered and the other women were apprehended but this one stole a car and made a run for it.

"Is she armed?" Abby asked.

"We're not sure. One of the other women had a gun but we're not sure about the escapee. Treat her as an armed escaped convict."

"Roger," Abby said, "giving chase."

Abby peeled out and entered the highway with her lights flashing and siren screaming. Other drivers quickly moved out of the way giving the police the right of way. Abby now had the open road ahead of her and she could see the red lights of the car she was pursuing. She looked at her speedometer and realized she was way above the safe driving limit. At this speed a bump in the pavement could send her cruiser flying. She was in the process of deciding to stand down, when she saw the red lights ahead of her become airborne and then she heard a loud bang. The fleeing driver had lost control sending her vehicle into the air. It crashed back onto the highway and burst into flames. Abby called it in to dispatch and asked for the fire brigade.

"Ambulance?" dispatch said.

"Yes. But I think it's too late for them."

"You were smart to back down," Jack told her later.

"I want to be a good cop," she said, "that means not risking my life unnecessarily."

"I heard it on the radio," Jack said, "that woman was part of a trio who robbed a bank in which two people lost their lives. They were serving life without parole when they broke out."

"Okay. Change of conversation," Abby said. "You don't talk about the Indian side of your ancestry."

"I don't need to. Just pick up a history book. Although history books don't give a full picture of them."

"That's why I want you to talk about them," Abby said.

Jack was silent, allowing his thoughts to wander. Then he smiled and told Abby "do you remember that joke I told about the chief who was riding while his woman was walking?"

"I do," Abby said, "but what does it mean in relation to your ancestors?"

"I have no idea."

"Well, if that chief were anything like you," Abby said, "he would have given his 'hoss' to the woman."

"Maybe."

The two women who were captured were sent back to prison with extra time added on. Jack thought it was ridiculous since they were already in for life without a chance at parole.

He was sitting at his desk preparing an invoice for an insurance company, for the work he did breaking up an 'accident for money' gang. It was the last scam they pulled that caused the insurance companies to decide enough was enough. They were going to fight back. A motorist was stopped at a light behind a car that had its rear end raised in the air. The light changed to green and the front car took off and stopped suddenly in the intersection. The car behind him braked hard but he hit the stopped car. The damage to the stopped car was just a cracked tail light which cost a few dollars to repair. The driver of the second car reported it to his insurance company. The insurance company, however, received a bill from the driver of the lead car. That driver put in a claim for severe damage to his car, a claim for severe injuries and a claim for lost wages. The company decided to fight back and hired Jack to investigate.

Jack interviewed the driver who caused the accident and when the man told him what had happened, he knew it was a scam. Jack gave the insurance company high marks for fighting back instead of just paying the claims. He went to work. The paperwork from the insurance company gave him the names and addresses of the claimant, the doctor who signed off that the man was severely injured and the lawyer who was handling the claim. Jack suspected all three men were faking it and he set out to prove it.

His first stop was the claimant who lived in a rundown part of the city. His name was Phillip Greenfield and a quick check showed him as a petty thief who served time and was unemployed.

Jack arrived at the man's residence to find a dilapidated three-story building with peeling paint and the front door unlocked. A hand scrawled sheet pinned to the wall showed Greenfield lived on the second floor in apartment 2A. Jack went up the stairs and knocked on 2A.

A voice said, "Who's it?"

"Jack Peregrin,"

"What you want?"

"I would like to speak to Mr. Greenfield."

"He ain't here."

"Do you know when he'd be back?"

"No. What you want with him?"

Through the unopened door Jack explained he was representing the insurance company to verify Mr. Greenfield's claim.

"Put your number and address under the door so he can call you later."

Jack slipped his card under the door and left. An hour later his phone rang and when he answered a male voice said, "you the dick working for that insurance company?"

"Yes. I represent Mutual Insurance."

"Okay. What'd you want to know?"

"Is this Phillip Greenfield?" Jack said.

"Yeah," the voice said, "you want to know about my claim I'll stop by your office." Then the phone went dead.

Jack had given his card with his address and based on the conversation he just had he knew what to expect. And he was not surprised. One hour later his office door swung open and three men hustled in. Jack opened the top right hand drawer of his desk and pretended to be searching for something so when they approached he looked up with the drawer half opened and his hand in it.

"You." one of them consulted the card in his hand, "you, Peregrin?"

"Yes. Jack Peregrin. And you are?" Jack knew exactly who the man was but pretended otherwise.

"Name's Greenfield. I'm the guy with the claim you're interested in."

"Oh, yes, Mr. Greenfield," Jack said, "just a routine investigation. Your doctor reported that the accident may have maimed you for life. The company just wanted to confirm this."

"Well, the doc is right but as you can see, I made a complete recovery. But I was hurt bad."

"I'm glad for you," Jack said. "Tell me a little bit about the accident. It was not reported to the police so we have no official proof."

"Oh, it's proof you want. Happy to oblige." Greenfield reached under his jacket and pulled out a gun and that was his mistake. In a flash Jack withdrew his hand from his desk drawer and his gun was in it and pointed at Greenfield.

"Stop," Jack shouted. Greenfield didn't stop so Jack shot the wrist of the hand holding the gun. Greenfield screamed and held up his shattered wrist which no longer held his gun. The other men went for their guns but Jack thundered at them. "You'll both be dead before you can get your guns out. Put your hands on your heads and kneel. You so much as twitch and I will shoot you."

Jack called the police and requested an ambulance for the bleeding Greenfield. He told the cops to frisk the kneeling men because they both had weapons. The police took statements from everybody including Jack and the ambulance carried Greenfield away to the hospital. A check showed the three men were not licensed to own the guns.

One of the cops said to Jack, "you're one hell of a shot. At the Academy they teach us to aim for the mass. You went after a very small target."

"I didn't want to kill him," Jack said, "and actually, I missed. I was aiming for the gun."

CHAPTER 5

Jack sent his report and an invoice to the insurance company. They denied Greenfield's claim and sent a check to Jack for his work. But he wasn't done. The industry was tired of fraudulent claims and decided to do something about it. The police did not have the manpower to investigate the claims so they hired Jack. and he decided to go after the head of the snake, which was the fraudulent doctors and lawyers who were behind the fraud.

Jack knew the job was bigger than he could handle alone so he made a proposal to Abby. it

"You want me to quit my job and come work for you?" she said when he approached her.

"No, no," he said, "I don't want you to quit. Just take a leave of absence. Hear me out."

His proposal was that Abby apply for a leave of absence from her job. He told her he would accompany her to talk to her captain about it and only the captain would know the real reason for her leave. Officially she would be on leave to care for a sick relative who would remain unnamed.

"With your law enforcement background, you would be a big help to me, and you would help put an end to a fraud that's costing all of us in the end. The insurance companies raise our premiums to cover their increased costs." he told her. "Don't say no immediately. Just think about it."

As he was leaving for his office the next day, Abby said to him, "stop by Headquarters at four o'clock. I've made an appointment to sit down with Josh Murray. That's my captain."

"Okay, great," Jack said, hugging her, "I'll be there."

Two days later a new desk was delivered to Jack's office. I was Abby's. She was now part of the team that would wage war against a corrupt gang of frauds.

"I haven't bought you a chair because I want you to pick out the one you would like," Jack said.

"Let me try yours," she said sinking into his desk chair. "I like this. It's very comfortable."

"Okay," he said, picking up his phone, "it will here later today. In the meantime, use mine. I have to stop by to see the lawyer who is my contact with the insurance people." He hesitated and added, "come with me. That way I don't have to repeat my conversation to you and you might have some ideas of your own."

"Right, Boss," she said and threw him a salute.

"No, no," he said, "I'm not your boss. We are equals in this endeavor. It might turn out you're more equal than me."

Jack had met Daniel Grisham, the lawyer for the insurance companies, before.

"I wasn't aware you had a partner," Grisham said, holding Abby's hand a little longer than necessary Jack thought, "delighted."

"She's a state trooper," Jack said with emphasis, "on loan to me. And the lady of my dreams." He thought he might as well throw that out. Sort of marking Grisham's boundaries.

Abby smiled at Grisham and did her Spocklike raising of one eyebrow at Jack. It still puzzled him how she did that.

They left Grisham's office armed with a file of everything that was known about the ring that operated the insurance fraud. As they pulled up to their office a delivery truck pulled up behind them. Abby's chair had arrived.

The men carried it up, removed the plastic it was wrapped in and adjusted it to suit her. Jack tipped them and sent them on their way. He removed every sheet of paper in the file and made copies for Abby.

"So, partner," he said, "ready to rid the world of insurance fraud?"

"I don't know about the world," she said, "but I'm ready to start with this small corner of it."

They both studied the file, going through it with a high degree of thoroughness. Jack stopped and leaned back in his chair as he studied Abby whose eyes were fixed on the sheets in front of her. She must have felt the weight of his eyes on her since she looked up.

"Rule number one," she said, "no staring at your partner. It's disconcerting."

"Noted," Jack said, "no staring."

"Let me amend that," she said, "no staring during office hours. At any other time, it's very okay. It might even be encouraged."

"Again, noted," Jack said. "Where do you think we should start?"

"I say we start with the doctors," Abby said.

"Agreed," Jack said. "Let's go through the list and pick one."

They picked the doctor who was the busiest with examinations of claimants and whose name appeared on most of the claims. Before contacting him they drove out to his office to see where he was located to get a handle on his practice. Doctor Joseph Shepard's office was in a stand-alone two-story building in an affluent part of the city. From the outside it appeared as if the good doctor occupied the entire building.

"Okay," Jack said, "let's go back to the office and find out who owns the building. My sense tells me the building is owned by the doc himself. Very luxurious looking building in an upscale neighborhood. Must be worth a pile."

"If you mean money, I agree," Abby said.

"Of course, money," Jack said, "what else could I mean?"

"Well, there is crap," Abby said.

"Did they teach you that at the Academy?" Jack said.

"Hell, no," Abby retorted, "I learned that in the 'hood."

"Oh, boy," Jack said, "I can see I chose the right partner."

"You mean partner in business or partner in life or partner..."

"Okay, okay," Jack said holding up his hand, "I should know better than to go head to head with a law enforcement officer."

Abby turned away so Jack could not see her smiling.

CHAPTER 6

Doctor Joseph Shepard was a prominent orthopedic surgeon with a large practice. His specialty was treating people who had suffered severe injuries due to accidents. No one questioned his diagnoses and treatments. Until now. Jack and Abby put their heads together and came up with a plan to out the good doctor. First things first. Jack bought a burner phone so his calls could not be traced.

A call went to the office of Doctor Joseph Shepard and when the receptionist answered a man by the name of Anthony Daniels requested an appointment with the doctor.

"I'm sorry," the receptionist said, "but Doctor Shepard won't be free for new patients for another four months."

"That's too bad," Daniels said, "I was in an accident and my lawyer said I should get a report from Doctor Shepard."

"Why do you need a report from Doctor Shepard?"

"I'm making a claim to an insurance company," Daniels said.

"Oh, I see," the receptionist said, "who is your lawyer?"

"Attorney Frank Thornton," Daniels said.

"Did you say Thornton? Hang on," she said.

After a short wait she came back on the line, "the doctor can squeeze you in tomorrow at ten. He's very busy so don't be late." Then she was gone.

"How did it go?" Abby asked Jack later that evening.

"Very well," Jack said, "Doctor Shepard will see me, no, Anthony Daniels tomorrow at ten, sharp."

"You remember what Shakespeare had Mark Anthony say about mischief." Abby remarked.

"Yes, I do," Jack replied, "and it will be afoot big time."

Daniels arrived for his appointment at exactly ten o'clock. The receptionist handed him a form for him to fill in with his name and address and the reason for his visit. He did as he was told and handed it back to her.

She looked it over and said, "okay, Mr. Daniels the nurse will take your vitals in a minute and then the doctor will see you."

The receptionist was spot on. In a minute exactly, a nurse stood at the entrance to the waiting room and called out, "Mr. Daniels."

His vitals were good. The nurse told him the doctor would be in to see him in a couple minutes. She left, closing the door behind her.

The next person to enter the examination room was Doctor Shepard with his hand out to greet Jack.

"So, Mr. Daniels," he said, "what seems to be the problem?"

Jack told him he was in a car automobile accident and he hurt his back. He was making a claim to the insurance company and his lawyer advised him to have the doctor examine him and write up a diagnosis and treatment plan.

"So, here I am," Daniels said.

"Okay. Let's get started. Take off your shirt, please."

The doctor used his fingers to probe Daniels's back and after a couple minutes of pushing and tapping his back, declared that Daniels had a herniated disc in his lower back and he was sure it was caused by the accident. When Daniels asked why he did not order an X-ray or MRI the doctor's manner changed. He became brusque and informed Daniels that it was not necessary and what's more he was the doctor and Daniels was the patient. He said he would forward a report to the lawyer and they would decide on a treatment after they knew how much the insurance would pay. In the meantime, Daniels should take it easy. Shepard stood and left the room, Daniels was dismissed.

"What did the doctor tell you?" Abby asked.

"He said I have a herniated disc in my lower back caused by the accident. I should take it easy and he would work out treatment after we know how much the insurance company would pay."

"How was his bedside manner?"

"Good, until I asked why he was not ordering X-rays or MRI"
"In other words, how dare you question him," Abby said.
"Exactly."
"You're up, Mrs. Daniels," Jack added.

Doctor Shepard's office phone rang and when the receptionist answered a woman by the name of Violet Daniels was on the other end.

"Can I help you?" the receptionist said.

"Sure. Name is Violet Daniels. Doctor Shepard seen my husband because he had an accident. What he told my husband can't be right. I think there's something fishy going on."

"You say you're Mrs. Daniels?"

"That's what I said," Violet said.

"I think you need to speak to Doctor Shepard about this," the receptionist said.

"Sure, Ducky. Tell him to call me. You got my number. Same as my husband's."

"Doctor Shepard is very busy," the receptionist said, "I'm not sure when..." The line went dead.

Jack was standing next to Abby as she clicked off the call.

"You done good, Ducky," he said. "I think you missed your calling."

"Now we wait," Abby said. "If Shepard is scamming the insurance companies, he'll call back. I expect to hear from him soon."

Soon was one hour later. The burner phone rang and Abby picked it up and pushed the answer button. It was Doctor Shepard.

"Is this Mrs. Daniels?"

"Sure is," Abby answered nodding to Jack. "Who's this?"

"Doctor Joseph Shepard."

"Oh, yeah. What can I do for you Doc?"

"You made a serious accusation to my receptionist. I'd like to know where you got the idea my diagnosis is wrong."

"Just a feeling. You didn't order any tests. Just sounds fishy to me"

"In my professional opinion they are not necessary," Shepard said.

"Well, in my professional opinion that sounds fishy," Mrs. Daniels said. " How can you tell what's wrong with my husband just by poking at his back? Sounds like you're running one of them fake pill mills you see on television."

"I can assure you, Mrs. er, Daniels, my diagnosis is based on my lengthy experience with the kind of injury your husband suffered. And furthermore..." Mrs. Daniels ended the call.

Abby looked at Jack, "the ball's in his court, now," she said, "let's see how he plays it. What address did you give?"

"An empty apartment on the South side. It is provided by the insurance company. It's furnished so we can use it when we think it's necessary to be there. If the doctor is going to make a run for us, it will be there. We should occupy it for a few days."

The doorbell rang and Abby got up to answer it. She looked through the peep hole and saw three men dressed in worked clothes. She held up three fingers to tell Jack they had three visitors.

Jack handed Abby her service pistol which she put in her pocket and went into the bedroom with the door opened just a crack.

Abby pulled the front door open. "Hello," she said, "can I help you gentlemen?"

"You, Miz Daniels?" one said.

"I am. What's this about?"

"Doc Shepard asked us to stop by and straighten out a problem you're having."

"Oh? What problem you're talking about?"

"Problem with your husband's diagnosis," one of them said.

"Oh, that," Mrs. Daniels said, "I think he's wrong. He made a mistake."

"The doc don't make mistakes."

"Well," Mrs. Daniels said, "come in and we'll talk about it."

They entered the apartment and one of them made the mistake of bringing a gun out his pocket. But Abby was ready. In a flash a gun appeared in her hand and in one motion she brought it down on the gunman's arm. His gun flew out his hand and he dropped to his knees holding his arm and screaming.

"You broke my arm," he yelled.

"I know,:" she said. "You were going to shoot me, weren't you?"

By this time Jack had emerged from the bedroom with his gun in his hand pointed at the other two. He moved it back and forth showing he was willing to shoot either one who made an attempt to go for a gun.

"Well now," Jack said, "let us sit down and discuss our favorite doctor. I gather you men work for him."

"We got nothing to say."

"That's too bad," Abby said, "Your friend needs medical attention and the more you refuse to cooperate the longer it will take for him to get to the emergency room. Look, his arms is already beginning to swell up."

"Oaky, okay," one of them said, "what'd you want to know?"

CHAPTER 7

"First, I want you to put your hands in your pockets and take out your guns by the barrels," Jack said, "I want to see your hands around the barrel if just one finger slips towards the trigger, my wife and I will put holes in your heads." They did as they were told and held the guns by the barrels with the triggers away from them.

"Now, put them on the table," Jack said, "be careful of what I said about your fingers and the triggers." Abby gathered the guns and took them into the bedroom.

"I think you should know, if you do walk out of here it will be without your guns," Jack told them.

"You're gonna steal our guns?"

"Not at all. Call it a donation to our gun collection. Now about Doctor Shepard."

"We really don't know Doctor Shepard," one of them said.

"What's your name?" Jack said

"I'm Lenny, he's Bob and the guy with the broken arm is Jessie."

"Okay. Tell me about Doctor Shepard's game."

"We don't know no Doctor Shepard," Lenny said.

"You're using two negatives and that means..." Jack stopped when he saw Abby shaking her head and waving her arms.

She was telling him, *"these men are thugs. They probably never finished school and you're talking grammar with them."*

"Lenny bore that out when he said, "I don't understand what you're talking about. We don't know no doctor by that name."

"So why are you here?" Jack said.

"We do work for a guy name of Mortis and he told us to come over here and scare Mrs. Daniels for the doctor."

"His name is Mortis? What's his first name, Rigor?"

"So, you know him," Lenny said. Jack looked at Abby and she heaved her shoulders.

"You got a call from this Mortis guy who told you to come over here and scare my wife."

"That's it. I swear on my mother's grave."

"Well," Abby said, "a man who swears on his mother's grave must be telling the truth. How about you, Bob."

"Oh, my mama ain't dead. But if she was dead I'd swear on her grave."

"Okay," Jack said, "get out of here. Better get your friend to a hospital or he might lose that arm. And you can report to your boss that you failed."

After they left Abby said to Jack, "Rigor Mortis?"

"Obviously not his real name," Jack said. "If your last name were Mortis would you name your son Rigor?"

"I might," she said, "if I wanted to snub my nose at society."

"This will get back to Shepard," Jack said, "we have to be prepared for him to up the ante."

Jack and Abby decided to stay where they were for a few more days to see what the doctor planned for them next and it came the next day.

Abby was returning to the apartment from a grocery shopping trip when a car bumped the SUV she was driving. They had rented the SUV for its size and power. When she got bumped she knew this was coming from the shady doctor so the game was on. She sped up crossed the grassy median and came up behind the car that bumped her. She returned the favor by bumping them. They tried to get away but their car was no match for the SUV. She pushed them until they came to a bridge then she sped up to come alongside and squeeze them against the bridge railing Their car stalled. Abby stopped with the SUV jamming the other car against the railing. Shots rang out from the car but went wide. They were pinned with the passenger side against the rail and the SUV against the driver side. They could not open their doors. They were trapped. Abby stood behind them and methodically shot out the rear window and all the other windows. There were three men in the car and they were all cowering down on the floor afraid of being shot.

"Throw your guns out now," she shouted, or I'll put a bullet in your gas tank and cause an explosion." She wasn't sure an explosion would occur but they weren't chancing it. The guns came tumbling out.

"Who sent you?" she shouted. When no answer came she said, "I'm counting to five and if you don't start talking, I will start shooting at your gas tank. One, two..."

"Hold it," came from the car. "Our boss sent us."

"Your boss? Any chance his name is Rigor Mortis?" There was no reply from the car.

"I'm resuming the count," Abby said, "three..."

?No. Wait," came from the car. "Yeah, that's his name but it ain;t his real name."

"Where can I find Mr. Mortis?" Abby said. There was no reply.

"Four," she said.

"Okay. We don't know where he's at because we get our orders by phone. But we know somebody who would know."

"This snake has many heads," Jack said when Abby related her run in on the bridge. He dialed the number Abby was given. James Overton.

When the call was answered, "Mr. Overton," Jack said, "I need to get hold of Rigor Mortis."

"Who?"

"Your man, Rigor Mortis."

"Is this some kind of joke

"No Joke, Mr. Overtone," Jack said, "Doctor Shepard is in peril and I need to find Mortis."

"Peril? What kind of peril?" Overton asked, "and who are you?"

"Who I am is not important," Jack said. "Your friend is in grave danger and we have to act immediately."

"His real name is Francis King. And he is usually at the Sunrise Market on Storrow Drive. He owns it. He calls himself Rigor Mortis because he thinks it's funny."

"Well, I would laugh but I don't have the time." Jack said and ended the call.

He turned to Abby, "Rigor Mortis and Francis King are one and the same. He owns the Sunrise Market on Storrow."

"Okay," Abby said, "we have to go shopping."

CHAPTER 8

Jack and Abby did a drive by the market to scout out the area. They parked and went on foot to the store taking note of how much traffic was on the sidewalk. There was a gap between two buildings and through this gap they saw there was an alley behind the stores. The alley was as wide as the street and there were cars there. While Abby waited on the sidewalk, Jack drove the car down the alley and parked near a door with SUNSHINE scrawled on it. Then he walked out of the alley and joined Abby on the sidewalk. They entered the shop and Abby grabbed a shopping basket from the pile near the door. Jack asked an employee, stacking shelves, for Mr. King. He was told Mr. King was in his office in back.

"I can get him for you," the employee said.

"No. That's okay," Jack said, "we'll catch him later."

There were two doors in the back of the store. One was a regular sized door marked PRIVATE and another much larger with employees pushing carts through it. They surmised the smaller door was to the office. It was at the end of an aisle with hardware. Jack and Abby pretended to be looking for something and when the aisle cleared, they pushed through the door and entered the office. King looked up from his computer and was about to tongue lash the employee who had disturbed him when he saw the strange couple standing there. And the man had a gun pointed at him.

"Move your hand away from your desk phone," Jack said, "and take your cell phone out of your pocket and give it to me."

When King hesitated Jack said, "do it now or I will put a hole in your head."

King did as he was told. "I don't have any money here in the office," he said, "all the money is in the registers."

"I'm not here for your money, Mr. Mortis," Jack said.

"What did you call me?" the man said.

"Mortis," Jack said, "your name is Rigor Mortis, isn't it?"

"I think here he's known as Francis King," Abby said.

"Tell me, Mr. Mortis er King," Jack said, "if we open that back door would an alarm sound?"

"Uh, er, Yes," King answered.

"Really. Let's go check it out. Move."

When they got to the door Jack noticed it was an ordinary door with no sign alerting people that an alarm will sound.

"You lied to me Mr. King, You shouldn't have done that," Jack said preparing to shoot him.

"Hold it Tony," Abby said, "I'm sure Mr. King didn't mean to lie."

"You're lucky my wife has a soft heart," Jack said. "That's my car. Get in and we'll have a long talk, you and us, Rigor Mortis. Where did you get that name?"

When they were all comfortably seated, Jack and King in front and Abby in back with a gun to King's head, Jack said, "do you know who we are?"

King shook his head. "I don't know who you are. All I know is you're robbing me."

"Wrong answer," Jack said. "Does the name Doctor Shepard mean anything?" No answer from King who was now sweating. He was beginning to realize this was not a plain robbery.

"How about Daniels?" Jack said, "it should ring a bell. Your people tried to kill us twice."

Jack was watching King's face and saw his eyes grow wide when he heard the name Daniels.

"Oh, the second gang never reported back. Guess what Rigor Mortis, here we are alive and kicking. We're going to punish you so badly you'll never send anyone else after us. And your patron Doctor Joseph Shepard is going down."

Jack started the car. "I think you should allow him to say goodbye," Abby said.

"Goodbye?' Jack said, "oh yes, to the good doctor, of course."

Jack took out Kings phone and found the doctor's number in his address book. "This must be a private number," Jack said pushing the button to dial the number.

"When he answers, say exactly, 'I'm calling to say goodbye,' and hang up. Anything else and you're a dead man."

"Nicely done," Jack said, " but I think he'll call you back."

He put the phone on the dashboard and smashed it with his gun. "He's going to sweat because he has no idea what you meant."

"What do we do about our guest, here?" Abby asked,

"I don't know, Violet," Jack said.

"What do you think we should do?"

"Well, we can't let him go. We could shoot him. After all he did send people to kill us."

"No, I didn't," King spoke up, "I sent them to just scare you."

"Why? You don't even know us," Jack said.

"When your wife threatened Doctor Shepard he got scared she was going to the authorities."

"Yeah," Jack said, "insurance fraud is a multi-million-dollar business. We're moving."

"To where?" King said.

"I don't know yet but it will be someplace where you can't keep sending people to hurt us."

Jack stopped in front of the police station.

"Why are we stopping here?" King asked.

"I'm turning you over to the police. We have enough evidence to prove you sent people to kill us. That's attempted murder."

"What? You can't do that." King said.

"Watch me," Jack said,. "I'm doing the police a favor. I'm bringing in a man who was involved in a murder for hire scheme."

Abby leaned on her captain to quietly find out what the local police were doing about the man Jack brought in.

"They have him locked up," she told Jack, "and some of his goons have flipped. To save their own asses they are talking and implicating the man they knew as Rigor Mortis"

Unfortunately for King he was housed in the same building as a man who blamed him for his problems with the police. The man was a thief and after he burgled a store, King alerted the police to where he was hiding. The man swore vengeance on King and waited for an opportunity to avenge himself. He served his time but after his release he went back to his old profession of burglarizing homes. He was caught again and was put in the same holding building as King, to await his trial. He could not believe his luck when he saw King being escorted into the building. After the guard left he went up to King and tapped him on his shoulder. King turned and his eyes went wide when he saw his old nemesis.

"Remember me?" the man said.

"What you want?" King said.

"This," the man said and brought his fist in an uppercut straight to King's jaw. This was a big man and he put all his weight into the punch. King's head snapped back and he fell backwards hitting his head on a bench. Other guards restrained the hitter while an ambulance was called in but by the time the ambulance arrived King had taken his last breath. He was hit with such force that when he hit his head on the bench he immediately went unconscious and never recovered.

"King's dead," Jack said, "he died when he was attacked by another prisoner."

"I don't wish ill on anyone," Abby said, "but I have no tears for that man."

"Me neither," Jack said, "but our plan was to use him to bring down Shepard. Now, it's back to square one."

"I think it's time Anthony Daniels checks in with his doctor," Abby said, "to find out what could be done for his herniated disc."

CHAPTER 9

Jack received a call from Mutual, the insurance company he was working for, telling him they had received a claim from Anthony Daniels for an exorbitant amount of money. The claim stated Mr. Daniels had suffered extensive damage to his spine and would require an untold amount of surgery and physical therapy before he was made whole. And maybe he would never be made whole.

Jack's response was, "stall. Do not pay any money. We're working on it. Anthohy Daniels does not exist except for our investigation."

He then called Doctor Shepard's office. "This is Anthony Daniels," he said, "I'm calling to find out what the doctor had decided about my treatment."

"Mr. Daniels," the receptionist said, "please hold."

The hold was a full five minutes and she returned to tell Daniels, "I'm sorry, the doctor cannot make a recommendation until he has heard back from your insurance company." Then she was gone.

"He is not going to hear from the insurance company," Jack told Abby, "because I told them to stall."

"In my opinion," Abby said, "you should tell them to okay it but not pay it. That puts the ball back in the doctor's court."

"Did anyone ever tell you you're a smart chick?" Jack said.

"If I had a nickel for every time someone told me that, I'd be a rich woman" Abby replied.

"And humble too," Jack said.

"Why hide your bushel...? Well, you know what I mean," she said.

One week later Daniels received a call from Shepard telling him to come in to discuss his treatment.

"Do you think we should move back into the apartment?" Abby asked.

"Yes. That would be a good idea," Jack said.

His appointment was set for ten o'clock on a Thursday morning and Jack kissed goodbye to Abby and took off.

Ten minutes after he left, the doorbell rang. Through the security hole Abby saw a well-dressed man of medium height carrying a briefcase. She opened the door as far as the security chain would allow and asked the man to state his business. He said he was an investigator working on behalf of Doctor Shepard and just needed a couple minutes of her time.

"Just a minute," she said, "I was about to use the powder room. I'll be right back."

She closed the door and went into the bedroom, opened the drawer of her night table and took out her gun. She put it in the pocket of the robe she was wearing. She hesitated thinking she should get dressed but decided the robe over her pajamas was best for hiding the weapon. She opened the front door and invited the man in.

"Please, be seated," she said, "you said something of doing an investigation for Doctor Shepard?"

"Yes, Mrs. Daniels," he answered, "my name is Jonathan Peters and I'm a private investigator. The doctor has asked to ascertain certain things about you."

"What certain things? My husband is right now keeping an appointment with the doctor."

"Yes, I know," Peters said, "the doctor has reason to suspect you and your husband are not who you seem to be."

"Why do you say that?" Abby said, "my husband had an automobile accident in which he was severely hurt. Doctor Shepard is the one who diagnosed him as having injured his spine I don't understand any of this."

"Mrs. Daniels," he said, "we believe you have ulterior motives and I'm here to learn what they are. It's very strange the insurance company approved your husband's treatment but gave no monetary value on his claim."

"You're not a private investigator, are you?"

"Well let's just say I'm private," Peters said, "and I want you to call the company and tell them you had made a mistake."

"And if I don't?"

"That won't be wise. Most men would not beat up a woman. I'm not most men."

"I take that as a threat to my life," Abby said. "What's in your briefcase?"

"I'll show you," he said opening the case and taking out a gun. But Abby was prepared.

As soon as he reached for his briefcase, Abby put her hand in her pocket and when his gun cleared his briefcase her gun was already in her hand.

"I think you came here to kill me," she said and fired. She was aiming for the gun which flew out of his hand taking two fingers with it.

"Bitch" he screamed, "you goddamned bitch you shot me in my hand."

He was holding up his hand as blood was dripping from it. Abby pointed her gun at him.

"Stay right where you are," she said, "I'm calling the police. They will bring an ambulance for you."

The police arrived to find Peters sitting on the floor with his bloody hand in front of him.

"This man tried to kill me," Abby said, "his gun is over there."

"Well, well," one of the cops said, "John Robles. Finally met your match."

"Do you know this man?" Abby said.

"Oh, yes," the cop said, "every cop in the district knows him. He's an enforcer for the mob and we've been trying to nab him for ages. Ma'am you did us a favor. But, to tell the truth, it would have been better if your aim was better."

"My aim was perfect," Abby said, "I wasn't trying to kill him. I just wanted to get his gun so he didn't kill me. Unfortunately, the gun took a couple fingers with it."

"Pity," the cop said. The ambulance arrived for Peters or rather Robles. They searched the area and found the two fingers but they were too smashed to be of any use.

Robles was handcuffed to the stretcher and they took him out.

"What's going to happen to him?" Abby asked.

"He's going to the hospital for treatment," the cop said, "and his next stop will be a prison for a very long visit. We have many warrants out on him for murder."

Jack was sitting in an examination room when the doctor entered.

"Mr. Daniels," he said, "how are you feeling?"

"Fine," Jack answered.

"Your insurance company approved your treatment but neglected to award a dollar amount. I can't proceed with treatment until we clear that up." He was pressing against Jack's back as he spoke.

"The good news is your problem hasn't got worse. We'll be in touch." He left the room.

"Yes, we will," Jack said to the empty room while he was buttoning his shirt.

"There is something I fail to understand," Jack said, "Shepard is losing people, but it doesn't seem to bother him."

"He's probably not aware that he is" Abby replied, "which works in our favor."

"Not quite," Jack said, "he sent that mob enforcer."

"He didn't know what was going down while you were there. The enforcer is in police lockup and Shepard would never want to be seen visiting him."

The police moved fast on Robles. He was tried and convicted in a hurry and sent off to a maximum security prison.

They had to take the DA into their confidence and he agreed not to call Mrs. Daniels to testify. He said they had so much on Robles her testimony was not needed, The news reports claimed a Mrs. Daniels, an ordinary housewife brought him down. It never got out that ordinary housewife was a state cop who had won several medals for her marksmanship.

CHAPTER 10

Jack and Abby decided to let Shepard stew for a while and turned their attention to Attorney Frank Thornton who was up to his neck in this fraud. Daniels went back to see him to find out where his claim stood.

"We're in good shape," Thornton said, "the insurance company has approved your claim but they have not yet assigned a dollar value. Patience, my friend."

"The doctor said he can't start my treatment until he knows how much the insurance will pay." Daniels said.

"I don't know why they're holding up," Thornton said. "Everything seems cut and dry. Maybe we're asking too much."

"I thought the amount we're asking is based on how much my treatments would cost," Daniels said.

"Yes, yes, of course," Thornton replied. "How is your back?"

"Fine," Daniels said, "I think Doctor Shepard is more concerned than I am."

"That's the way he is," Thornton said.

Jack told Abby he could not sense any concern in Thornton about committing fraud. They needed a break-through to bring him down. And it came from an unexpected source.

Thornton's office was one of six in a two-story building on a quiet side street. Over the weekend thieves broke into the building and burgled all the offices. On Sunday night Thornton received a call at home from the police. They wanted him to come down to his office that had been broken into.

Thornton arrived to find several police cars and the other tenants on the sidewalk in front of the building. He immediately went into his office to find, not only desks and filing cabinets open but his safe was standing open and the contents gone. He had a small amount of money in the safe but this was relatively unimportant. What was of the utmost importance were the files of his cases he was working on including insurance files going back over the last ten years. These files could send him to prison because they were details of the fraud he had committed.

He asked the police if they had any idea who the thieves were. They did not know who they were. Maybe their investigation might turn up somebody. This was bad news to the lawyer. He hoped the thieves would simply keep the money and toss the files.

A week after the robbery a call came into his office from someone claiming to have something of his and he was willing to sell it to Thornton. The caller said he would call back the next night with a price. He wanted time to see how much the articles were worth on the black market. Thornton knew the man had his files detailing the different frauds he had pulled. The man had used a burner phone to call so it was useless to try a trace. The information the man had could put him away for many years. The man said he would call the next night with a price for the files. There was nothing to be done except wait for the call. The call didn't come the next night nor three nights after. Thornton was in full panic mode. He began envisioning a knock on his door with the police entering with handcuffs.

The call came six days later and the caller told Thornton he had read through all the files and realized how hot they were.

"Your fraud could get you thirty years," the man said, "but I'm a reasonable man. You can dodge prison if you pay me one hundred thousand and cut me in on any future cases. I keep the files as insurance."

Thornton's jaw dropped when he heard this. " I don't have that kind of money," he protested.

"Far as I can tell you been doing this for about ten years," the man said, "I'm sure you made more than that. I think you're lying. Take one day to think about it. I'll call you tomorrow." Then he was gone.

Thornton called his accomplice to report the theft. There was a long pause on the line and when he found his voice Shepard said, "is my name on any of those files?"

"Of course, your name is on the files," Thornton shouted, "you provided the medical reports."

"How many kinds of idiot are you?" Shepard said, "how could you allow this to happen?"

"Look, Shepard," Thornton said, "I wasn't such an idiot when you were hauling in the money. If I go down I'm taking you with me."

It was big news that thieves had hit the building that housed several prominent lawyers. The building housed so many lawyers it was known as the law building. When Jack heard about it he asked Abby to get information on the victims and she found out Frank Thornton's office was hit. She also found out the thieves made off with all the files in his safe.

"Why would he keep files in his safe and not a filing cabinet?" she said.

"He would keep them in a safe if they were files only he had access to." Jack said. "Those files are now in the hands of thieves. I think that lawyer and his doctor accomplice are on hot seats. They'll have to come up with a lot of money if they want to avoid prison. I think Daniels should get in touch and say he was sorry to hear about the burglary."

The thief called to set up the exchange. "We do it in the open," Thornton said, "and I want my files or no deal."

"Okay with me," the thief said. "That open air restaurant across from the park Make it three o'clock. Usually empty at that time."

Thornton was already sitting at a table with a brief case on the table when the thief arrived. He was a tall skinny man, bearded and bald. He looked around and saw a man sitting at a table with a briefcase.

He approached the man and sat down.

"You got the money?"

"Yes. In the briefcase. You got the files?"

"Yes. In this paper bag."

Thornton was about to open the briefcase when the thief stopped him.

"I want you to know we got company," he said, "a little insurance in case you try to pull something. See that man in the red shirt? He's with me. And that blue shirt and green shirt too. If you come up with anything other money from that case, they gonna shoot you."

Thornton opened the case and showed him the money in neat layers. The thief closed the case and pulled it to him then he passed the bag with the files over. The thief was satisfied. He nodded to his accomplices and they left.

"Nice doing business with you, counsellor," the thief said and turned to leave. Thornton saw an opportunity. He took a gun from his jacket pocket and hit the thief on his head. As he started to crumble to the ground Thornton grabbed the briefcase and ran. The thief was not dead and Thornton knew as soon as he revived he would come for him. The thief knew his office location and his phone number. But Thornton did not know the thief had made copies of the files.

CHAPTER 11

Thornton knew he had to disappear and fast. He stayed away from his office for two weeks and cancelled his phone service. He scoured news sources to learn what happened to the thief. There was a short piece in the papers of a man who was found lying on the ground in the open air restaurant. The man said someone attacked him and took his money but he did not see the attacker. He was hit from behind. Thornton wondered why the thief did not give up his name but he put it out his mind and carried on with his life and work. He rented office space on the other side of town and got a new phone service with a new number. He also started carrying his gun for which he had received a license two months ago. As the weeks passed, Thornton slowly began to relax thinking there wouldn't be any repercussions from his run in with the thief whose name he now knew to be Albert Senac.

One day a man whose left arm was encased in a cast as well as his left foot, limped into his office. The man told him he stopped by on the odd chance Thornton could see him. He would have phoned but he did not have the number. The man needed a lawyer because he was suing an insurance company who was balking at paying his claim for injuries he suffered as a result of a car accident.

"How did you get my name?" Thornton asked the man.

"My neighbor suggested you," he said.

"Who is your neighbor??

"His name is Albert Senac. Lives across the hall from me. He said you won a case just like mine two, three years ago."

Two, three years ago. That son-of-a-bitch made copies of my files.

Thornton told the man he was just leaving and he should come back the next day. As he drove he noticed a white Lincoln following him. As he thought about it, he had seen that Lincoln several times. This was more than a coincidence. He was being followed and he suspected it was that thief, Senac. He slowed down and allowed the Lincoln to pass him and as it drew adjacent to him the front passenger window rolled down and a man yelled at him, "you're a dead man, Thornton," and the car sped away. Thornton also sped up to catch up with the Lincoln and tucked in behind him. They were approaching an intersection and the Lincoln's right turn red light came on but he was behind another car so he had to wait to turn. Thornton moved into the left lane and sped up to be adjacent to the Lincoln. He had already taken his gun from the glove compartment and it was lying on the seat. Just as the Lincoln was beginning the turn, Thornton pushed the button to roll down his passenger window and took aim at Senac who was driving. He squeezed the trigger and the bullet smashed through the Lincoln's driver window. Thornton then hit the gas and kept on going.

The bullet smashed through the window but the glass changed its trajectory and it missed the driver. But it caused Senac to lose control and smash right into a tanker that was stopped at the red light. The Lincoln punctured one of the gas tanks and gasoline started spewing out and onto Senac's car which burst into flames as soon as the gas seeped onto the hot engine. The blazing car then caused the tanker to explode and heave itself into the air, falling back to settle on Senac's car and create a blazing inferno. The driver of the tanker was able to escape the burning wreck but not the people in Senac's car. All four of them died in the flames.

Very shortly the police had the entire area cordoned off while the fire fighters poured fire retardant foam on the blaze. Among the people who had gathered on the sidewalk was a man who approached a cop and told him he witnessed what happened and he knew who caused it.

"Obviously the car hit the tanker," the cop said.

"Yes, but that was because someone shot at the driver of the car," the bystander said.

"Are you sure about this?" the cop said.

"Yes," the witness said, "he shot that diver and took off but I got his tag number."

"Okay, wait here my captain is going to want to talk to you."

After the fire was out and the two vehicles were cold the ME and his team went to work combing through the wreckage.

"A witness said he saw a passing driver shoot at the dead driver," the captain said.

"Maybe a bullet was fired but it didn't kill the driver of that car," the ME said, "The hole in the window shows the bullet went in on an angle. And there are no bullet holes in any of the occupants of that car."

"Is it possible the bullet caused the driver to lose control and ram the tanker?" the captain said.

"That would be my guess," the ME said.

The accident was all over the news. The police reported an eye witness came forward and said he saw the accident. They did not divulge the witness's name nor did they mention he had seen a car speed away and had written down the license number of the car.

It didn't take the police long to trace the license number to Thornton. There was a knock on his door and he opened it to three uniformed officers.

"Mr. Thornton?"

"Yes. I'm Frank Thornton. What can I do for you, gentlemen?"

"We're investigating an accident that occurred earlier."

"Yes. It was all over the news," Thornton said, "one of the deceased was a friend of mine."

"Oh? Which one?"

"Albert Senac. I believe he was driving the car."

"We have a witness who says he saw you shoot at Mr. Senac," the cop said.

"Shoot at him? Why would I do that? He was a friend of mine."

"The witness said he saw the gun in your hand and there is a bullet hole in the driver window."

"A gun? No, no, I didn't have a gun in my hand. I had my phone in my hand and I waved to Al. I suppose a phone can look like a gun from a distance."

"What about the hole in the window?" a cop asked.

"I have no idea. Could have been from an earlier run in Al had," Thornton said, "I'm an attorney and I can't remember the number of times I had to get him out of bad situations. He ran with a rather unsavory crowd. It won't surprise me he had a run in with another guy who shot at him."

"Sir, do you own a gun?"

"I do but I keep it locked up in the glove compartment of my car."

The officer who did most of the talking looked at the others and they nodded.

"Okay, Attorney Thornton," he said, "sorry for the intrusion." They turned on their heels and left.

CHAPTER 12

Jack and Abby were relaxing on their patio after a great breakfast which Jack fixed. They were watching some ducks paddling along on the smooth surface of the lake that was one boundary of their property.

"What do you suppose is the real story behind that accident that killed four people?" Abby asked.

"I couldn't give you a reason why I think it, but I think Thornton is wrapped up in it." Jack answered.

"I didn't know men could have women's intuition," Abby said.

"This man could," he said, "and it comes from hanging out with you."

"It's again time for Anthony Daniels to consult with his attorney," Jack added.

Daniels called the number for Thornton only to be told the number was no longer in service. So, he drove to the office and found it empty. Thornton had moved and Daniels had no idea where he had moved to.

Abby found out from her captain the local police had Thornton in their sights. They knew he lied when he said he was just waving to Senac with his phone. A bullet had pierced Senac's window but missed his head. The bullet was found imbedded in the radio. They wanted Thornton's gun to check the barrel to see if the rifling matched the stripes on the bullet. But Thornton and his gun had disappeared.

After the police left Thornton's residence he assumed they did not believe him and sooner or later they were going to tie him to the accident. Four men had lost their lives and it made sense the police would do everything in their power to find who was responsible. Thornton thought his only recourse was to run. And he did. He owned a cabin in upstate Maine in a secluded area on a lake. The day after the visit by the police he withdrew a substantial amount of money from his account, loaded his car with necessities and headed to Maine.

He didn't know how long he needed to be there. He only knew he had to get away from the heat. He was sure no one knew of his cabin out there in the wilds of Maine so, it was a good place for him to hide out. But he was brought up short when he remembered his partner in crime, Doctor Shepard knew about the cabin. The two men had spent a glorious weekend fishing in the lake. He figured the police had no reason to question the doctor about his whereabouts. They had no reason to tie the two men together. Unless his copied files surfaced. If Senac had the files with him in the car, then they burned with him. But what if he gave the files to someone for safe keeping. Someone like his lawyer.

Before he arrived at the cabin, he stopped in the largest town and bought a burner phone. He needed to make calls from the cabin and didn't want them traced. His first call was the private number he had for Doctor Shepard.

"Where the hell are you?" Shepard said, "All hell's breaking out here."

"I moved," Thornton said. He didn't want Shepard to know he was in Maine. "Tell me what's happening. Anybody talk to you?"

"Nobody's talk to me yet," Shepard said, "but the insurance company contacted me looking for more details on the Daniels claim"

"Stall them," Thornton said and disconnected.

Unknown to Thornton, Senac had placed the copies of the files in a large envelope which he gave to his brother, John, with instructions for him to open the envelope should he, Albert, die under suspicious circumstances. Albert died in an accident but the police were investigating it as if there were more to it than just an accident. To John that was suspicion enough so he opened the envelope. The first page of the stapled documents was a letter telling John how he, Albert, came by the files and that John should use them to carry out what Albert failed to do. And that was to squeeze Thornton hard for every penny he could get.. The files John was holding in his hands were evidence of a fraud Thornton was running with insurance companies which could send him to prison for several years.

John read through the documents a second time to absorb the full extent of the fraud that had been going on for about ten years, and silently thanked his brother for this unexpected bounty. Albert had handed him a gift and he fully intended to make use of it. But he realized this was not going to be easy when he arrived at Thornton's office and found it empty. The police confirmed his suspicion that Thornton was in the wind. But John had information the police didn't and that Thornton was running an insurance fraud with an accomplice. And that accomplice was the well-known Doctor Joseph Shepard. To John's way of thinking all was not lost. He called Shepard's number to ascertain he was still around and when his receptionist answered, he hung up.

John Senac showed up at the office of Doctor Shepard asking to see the doctor. The receptionist told him the doctor does not see people without an appointment.

"Look, honey," John said to her, "if you value your job, just call him and tell him a man is out here with an important message form Frank Thornton."

She did as she was told and was looking at John as she listened to what her boss was telling her.

"Doctor Shepard is with a patient now," she said, "but he will see you in about ten minutes. Please have a seat in the waiting room."

Jack and Abby were at a loss as to Thornton's whereabouts. Daniels contacted Doctor Shepard to let him know the lawyer had disappeared and asked about his claim and his treatment. The doctor did not know where the lawyer was and was vague about his treatment. When Daniels asked about the status of his claim the answer he received was the claim was on hold.

"What does that mean?" Daniels asked.

"It means they have not committed a dollar amount for your treatment, yet," Shepard said.

"We know where Shepard is," Jack said, "we need to find Thornton. Why don't you contact your captain and ask if he has further information?"

"The police have an idea he is hiding out in a place he has in Maine," Abby said, "they leaned on the tax people and found out he pays taxes on a cabin on a lake in Maine. Probably bought with money from his fraud."

"Feel like making a trip to Maine?" Jack said, "Probably do some fishing while we're there."

"A trip to Maine, yes," Abby said, "fishing, no. Unless you bait my hook for me."

"Don't tell me the cream of the State Police is afraid a little worm." Jack said.

"They wouldn't bother me if they didn't squirm so much." Abby replied.

Thornton had just finished lunch when there was a knock on his front door. He opened it to his client Daniels and a woman.

"What? What, how," he stammered, "Mr. Daniels how did you find me?"

"It wasn't easy," Jack said, "we had to pull a lot of strings. And my name is not Daniels, I'm Jack Peregrin and this is Abigail Saunders. We're private investigators hired by the insurance companies you've been scamming for the last ten years."

Thornton's face fell. He just shook his head in defeat.

"Let me get dressed," he said.

"That's fine," Jack said, "I want you to come out of your bedroom with your hands in the air. If we don't see your hands up, we will both put holes in your head." For emphasis they both drew their weapons.

When it seemed to Jack, Thornton was taking a long time, he looked at Abby with a question in his eyes. She walked over to the bedroom door and listened with her ear against the door. There was no sound coming from the room. She gave the door a shove and they both stood aside with their guns trained on the opening. The room was empty. Then they saw the door that led to a small patio in the back. Then they heard an outboard engine revving. They ran to the door just in time to see Thornton running full out in a boat.

CHAPTER 13

Jack stared at the retreating boat and uttered one word, "unbelievable." Abby had no words.

"I have no words," she said.

"We're not far from the Canadian border," Jack said, "he may be aiming to sneak across."

"On foot?"

"No. He will run out of lake very soon so he'll hide the boat in the shallows and hide out in the woods until we leave. Then he would come back for his car and drive across the border."

"So, to foil his plan we need to set up housekeeping right here in this cabin."

"Exactly. Check on our food supply."

"It doesn't matter. One of us can go into town while the other stays here. We can outwait him. We're in a comfortable cabin while he's out in the woods with the bears and mosquitoes."

They had to wait just two days. They heard the faint sound of a motor in the distance but it cut off. They looked off in the distance across the water and saw the faint outline of a boat. As it got nearer they saw a man in it paddling as hard as he could. Abby drove their car back up the path and hid it among the trees and went back to the cabin to wait for Thornton with Jack. They turned off all lights in the cabin and waited in the dark for the owner to return. They watched as Thornton tied up to the dock and started to walk to the cabin with his gun in his hand. The cabin looked empty but he wasn't taking a chance.

Jack had positioned himself behind the drapes on the door that opened onto the back patio. He could see his quarry through a small gap. Thornton hesitated momentarily opened the door and entered with his gun hand extended. Jack brought his own gun down on the outstretched hand with as much force as he could muster. Thornton's gun flew out his hand while he grabbed his arm and dropped to his knees, all the while screaming at the top of his lungs.

He was still on his knees when he looked up at Jack and Abby standing in front of him with their weapons pointed at his head.

"You broke my goddamn arm," he said.

"Yes. I'm sure," Jack said, "I'll call an ambulance but first we need to talk."

"I don't have anything to talk to you about," Thornton said.

"Okay. Understood," Jack said, "but if that arm is not treated you might lose it. It will swell up for sure and sepsis might set in. A very painful death."

Abby was not entirely sure of the problems Jack was laying out but Thornton was believing it. To add proof to what Jack was saying. The arm was showing signs of swelling.

"The sooner we have our little talk," Jack said, "the sooner you can get medical help."

"What do you want to know?"

Jack looked at Abby. "Attorney Thornton," she said, "we've already established you've been defrauding insurance companies for many years. We'd like to know who your accomplice is."

"What proof do you have?" Thornton tried to talk his way out of his problem.

"We have plenty of proof. And isn't your arm hurting more by now?"

His arm was swelling up and the pain was becoming unbearable but he was sucking it up.

"You're both private," he said, "you can't arrest me."

"True," Jack said, "Abby?"

Abby walked outside and called her boss. When she explained where she was and what was going down he told her as of that very moment she was no longer a private detective but a police officer for the state of Maryland. He also told her he would contact the Maine state police and request their help.

Abby went back inside and found Thornton lying on the sofa holding his arm.

"I'm no longer private," she said to Jack and to Thornton, "I'm an officer of the State Police of Maryland."

"Aren't you out of your jurisdiction?" Thornton wheezed out.

"True, " Abby said. "Hold a minute. I think I hear sirens."

There was a knock on the door and Jack opened it to two uniformed officers from the Maine State Police. He introduced himself and Abby who showed them her badge.

"Came a long way," a Maine officer said.

"Yeah. This guy was trying his best to get up into Canada where we couldn't grab him without a lot of red tape."

"Can you give us some details of his crime? Your people in Maryland said you'd fill us in."

"Gladly," Abby said and gave a full report of Thornton's fraud.

"I'll be damned," the officer said, "that's why the insurance on my family vehicle is so high. The insurance companies raise our premiums to cover the money they pay out to these sleazebags. You're under arrest for insurance fraud."

"He needs medical attention," Jack said.

"As far as I'm concerned he can rot in hell," the officer said, "but I guess I will get an ambulance out here. You're lucky I'm sworn to uphold the law or I would let your arm swell up and drive you nuts with the pain."

A few minutes later they heard the siren of the ambulance coming up the path. The police didn't think it was necessary to restrain Thornton and that was their mistake.

The medics had him on a stretcher and as soon as they got him out the door he jumped off the stretcher and headed into the woods.

"Hey," the medic yelled.

"Stop or I'll shoot," one Maine officer shouted. Thornton didn't stop so the officer shot.

Thornton fell on his face. When they got to him the medic said, "I won't give two cents for his life, now. He has a broken arm and a shattered spine. He might as well be dead."

CHAPTER 14

Jack lost his partner when Abby went back on the force. The local outlets were full of the news about the attorney whom the police suspected was involved in that accident that killed four people and who was severely injured in a gun battle with the Maine State Police. Nothing was said about why the man was in Maine fighting it out with the cops up there. The story was obviously incomplete and the police in Maryland knew that reporters would continue to dig until the truth came out. And Jack decided to help things along. Without giving his identity and using a burner phone, he called police headquarters and told them to look into a rumor that Frank Thornton was deeply involved in an insurance fraud that netted him millions of dollars.

The doctors were able to fix Franks's broken arm but they said his spine was beyond repair. He would never walk again and was confined to a wheelchair for the rest of his life. The question that was left unanswered was why he tried to run when they were transporting him to a hospital in Maine. The rumor was he was trying to commit suicide by cop rather than face a lengthy prison sentence for something else. But no one knew what that something else was and Thornton was not talking.

Thornton, however, saw Shepard as the enemy. The man had profited immensely from the fraud and was now living free while he, Thornton, was condemned to a wheelchair. He dreamt of exacting revenge for this injustice. One way he could achieve this was to release his files to the police but he was afraid the doctor might use his position to squirm out of it. He wanted to see Shepard suffer like he was. But his options were limited. Unless he could sway John Senac, the brother of the now dead thief, over to his side. He was in a position to add to the details in the files thereby giving John solid leverage to blackmail Shepard for large sums of money. He had it in his power to bankrupt Shepard. The problem was he didn't know where Senac was.

He once heard someone say, the best way to hurt a rich man was to make him a poor man. He was going to turn Shepard into a poor man. He needed help and as he was wracking his brain to come up with someone who could help him he hit upon the detective whom he once knew as Anthony Daniels. The man was a private eye working for insurance companies. He searched his memory for a name and after a while came up with it. Jack Peregrin.

Jack was at his desk preparing an invoice for work he had done for a bank when the call came in. Caller ID showed NO ID but Jack was used to this. He was in the business in which people were reluctant to proclaim their identity. Some of his best clients refused to give their identities initially. He answered and was floored when the man who was calling gave his name. Frank Thornton. That was a person he never thought he would hear from.

"You surprise me, Mr. Thornton," Jack said.

"How so?" Thornton said.

"The last time we saw each other you tried to kill me and I you. But a Maine trooper put you in a wheelchair."

"True enough," Thornton said, "I need to hire you."

"To do what?" Jack said.

"I'll tell you that when I see you," Thornton said, "if you tell me where your office is located I'll come to you."

"But you're..."

"That's alright. I get around with a little help. Someone will drive me. I hope there's an elevator in your building."

"There is," Jack said, "but I have to give you fair warning. If you're coming here to harm me, don't bother I'll kill you before you can even twitch."

"No problem there, Mr. Peregrin. I don't even own a gun anymore. The police confiscated it. Please tell me what time is good for you."

At the appointed time there was a knock on Jack's door. He swung it open and stood behind it as Thornton wheeled himself in looking around the office.

"I'm here, Mr., Thornton," Jack said out from behind the door with his gun in his hand.

"I'm not armed," Thornton said, "as I said I want to hire you."

"I gather you would prefer to remain in your wheelchair," Jack said as he was removing one of the client chairs to make room for the wheelchair.

"I would. Yes." He replied.

"Now, then, what can I do for you, Mr. Thornton?" Jack said.

"To begin, I would like to dispense with the Mr. my name is Frank," Thornton said.

"Okay Frank, my name is Jack. Now, how may I help you?"

"I want to bankrupt one Doctor Joseph Shepard." Frank said.

Jack stared at the man not sure he heard him say what he thought he said.

"Did you say you want to put this doctor into bankruptcy?"

"That is correct. I have the means to do it but I need help."

"What means?" Jack asked.

"This," Frank said going through a bag in his lap and producing his files which he placed on the desk in front of Jack.

Jack took his time reading through the files. "These files indict you of insurance fraud, Frank," he said.

"Yes, and also Shepard." Frank said. "I'm totally paralyzed from the waist down what good would it be to put me in prison. I'm already in a prison. But Shepard is walking around free and clear. I want to bring him down."

"You don't need me to do that," Jack said, "just turn these files over to the police."

"That's not enough," Frank said, "I want him to suffer the way I am. If I could, I'd shoot the bastard. Even that might be too lenient. If I give these files to the police he might find a way to squirm out of it. I want to break him financially."

"What do you have in mind, Frank?" Jack said, "are you asking me to blackmail him?"

"No. I have someone else in mind for that. I want you find that person."

"Hold on," Jack said, "you want to hire me to find the man who will blackmail Shepard for you. Am I correct in this?"

"That's it in a nutshell." Frank replied

"I cannot condone blackmail and I won't aid and abet it," Jack said.

"Look at it this way," Frank said, "you would be righting a wrong done to me and you would help to bring down a sleazebag who has been bilking insurance companies who in turn make you pay high premiums."

"That is what the police do, Frank," Jack said. "My advice is turn the whole thing over to the police."

"Weren't you hired to get the goods on this doctor?"

"Yes. And on you," Jack said.

"Look at me. You've done your job. I'm in a prison I can never break out of. I would like to see Shepard in a similar prison."

"Who is it you want me to find?"

"I can't tell you that unless you agree to find him for me."

"Sorry, Frank," Jack said, "I can't do that. But I will do this for you. I will pretend this conversation never happened."

CHAPTER 15

"What do you think he will do?" Abby asked when Jack told her about Thornton's visit.

"He will eventually find an investigator who will find his guy. He made the mistake of telling me his real reason for wanting the man found. He won't make that mistake again."

"Or he could come across an investigator without your scruples,"

"Possible," Jack said.

What Thornton didn't know was that Senac was already putting the squeeze on Shapard.

John Senac was sitting in an examination room waiting for Doctor Shepard to make his appearance.

Shepard came bustling in. "I'm a busy man," he said, "so get right to it. I hear you have a message for me. "

"Yes, Sir," Senac said, "and I think it is very important. Here it is." He gave the files to Shepard whose face fell when he saw them.

"Where, uh, where did you get this?" he stammered.

"Doesn't matter," Senac said, "the important question for you is how much am I willing to sell them for."

"Blackmail," the doctor said.

"Don't say it like that," Senac said, "just look at it as a business deal."

"How much?"

"Well. first off they are not all for sale. You can buy a portion of them each time."

"You intend to blackmail me a little bit at a time," the doctor said.

"You have to decide what it's worth to stay out of prison." As he said this he reached over and took the files from Shepard.

"I could go to the police," Shepard said.

"Of course," Senac said getting up to leave, "good luck."

"Wait," Shepard said, "how much?"

Senac reclaimed his seat. "Your fraud was over a span of ten years. I'm a reasonable man. Go over your files and come up with how much you made on each fraud and pay me thirty percent of what you made. You can take your time to come up with the numbers. But be sure of one thing. If I suspect you're trying to cheat me the deal is off and you'd be hearing from the DA. I'll call you in three days. And tell your gatekeeper when she hears my name she put the call through. I don't want to hear any crap about how busy you are."

"Not only are you robbing me you're trying to humiliate me," the doctor said.

"Do you have any idea how much my insurance premiums have gone up because of scumbags like you, Doctor?" Senac said, "think about that while you run the numbers."

"How do I know you won't take my money and still go to the police?"

"You don't," Senac said, "but there is honor among thieves."

Frank Thornton could not find anyone to blackmail Shepard for him so he decided to do it himself. He called Shepard as a prelude to blackmailing him but got a surprise.

A hostile Shepard answered by saying, "What the hell do you want?"

"What do I want?" Thornton said. "I'll tell you what I want. I want money and I'm getting it from you."

"Sure. Line up," Shepard said.

"What do you mean by that?" Thornton said.

"You're a little late in the blackmail game. Somebody else is bleeding me because of your stupidity."

"Look Shepard I'm the one that's living in a wheelchair," Thornton said.

"I don't give a damn about you. I feel no responsibility for you being in a wheelchair. You're a stupid man and your stupidity put you in that wheelchair. Goodbye. Don't call me again."

Thornton ended the call with a smile on his face. He didn't have to do anything after all. He'll just sit back and watch somebody else bleed Shepard dry. It was almost worth being stuck in a wheelchair.

After Thornton left his office, Jack went into action. The files in Thornton's possession told the entire story of the insurance fraud he and Doctor Shepard ran for about ten years He wanted to know where Thornton lived so he followed him staying well back so as not to be made. Thornton's car stopped at a modest three-story apartment building on the other side of town. The driver got out and opened the trunk to retrieve the wheelchair. Then he went around to the passenger side and opened the door for Thornton. He helped Thornton into the chair and left him waiting on the side walk while he drove the car a little further on to a vacant parking space.

Jack was parked on a hydrant while he took in what was happening with Thornton. He stayed there until the driver came back and helped Thornton through the door and into the elevator. Jack left his car for a minute while he went up to the door and read the address board. Frank Thornton lived on the second floor in apartment 2A. He was returning to his car when he spied the meter maid hurrying to ticket his car. He jumped into it and drove away leaving her staring at the departing car.

"When do you plan to contact the DA?" Abby asked Jack.

"I'm not convinced those two men were the only ones conducting the fraud," Jack said, "my sense tells me there are other people involved. I have an idea how to smoke them out."

"Okay. Let me know if you need me," she said.

"I always need you," Jack said, reaching for her.

"Down boy," she said, "I am talking about the case."

"Oh, that," Jack said, feigning disappointment. "I'll let you know when I've formulated my plans."

"I know it's not possible but I wish you could leave Thornton out of it. It's almost like he has already paid the price for his crime. He has no hope of ever walking again."

"Going soft, on me are you?" Jack said.

"Maybe. I just feel a bit sorry for the man. I'm not excusing what he did and giving him a pass but he's lost both of his legs. In a perfect world that might be enough punishment."

"I hear you," Jack said, "and the DA might agree with you and ask the judge to fine him. I don't think prisons are set up to incarcerate people in wheelchairs."

Jack knew Thornton and Shepard were the principals in this criminal enterprise but he was thinking there were many other people who profited to a lesser degree and who should be made to pay.

CHAPTER 16

When Jack accepted this case he did due diligence on Doctor Shepard and discovered he was a wealthy man. His wealth came from his flourishing medical practice and from his real estate ventures. He owned a sizeable piece of the city in office buildings and malls. But his latest search showed a considerable reduction. It showed the doctor had to sell off a large portion of his real estate holdings and the proceeds could not be accounted for elsewhere. Jack wondered what was going on.

Jack traced down Thornton to see if he could shed some light on what was happening to Shepard.

"He's being blackmailed," Thornton said.

"You ..."

"No, not me. Someone else. When my office was robbed a thief took my files and I paid a lot of money to get them back. But the thief had copies which he gave to his bother for safe keeping. The thief died in that tanker crash but his brother had the files which he's now using to blackmail Shepard.

"Can I see those files again?" Jack said.

"You can have them," Thornton said, "I would like to wash my hands of this entire business."

Jack took the files to his office, poured himself a cup of coffee from the coffee maker he kept on a file cabinet, and sat down to study them. The files gave him a lot of detail about the fraud operation. He was right. There were other people who benefitted from it so, to bring down the operation he had to include all the minor players. He had a big job ahead of him and wished Abby was still working with him but she was at her post keeping the highways safe.

He made a list of the three people who stood out from the rest of the minor players. The first person on his list was Steven Jacobs with an address on the south side of town. Jack drove to the address and found himself in a seedy, rundown area. Many of the buildings were just shells but there were still some buildings that were occupied. He found the name Jacobs on the board and pushed the button.

"What you want?" greeted him.

"I'm looking for Steven Jacobs," Jack said.

"He ain't here."

"Do you know when he'll be back?"

"Who the hell knows? The cops took him. They may take him straight to jail," the voice said.

"Why?"

"They say he jacked a car. I dunno. Maybe he did, maybe he didn't. Always in trouble with the law"

"Can I come up to talk to you?"

"What for? Ain't got nothing to say. Go away."

Jack told Abby about his remote conversation with someone at Jacobs's address. It appears Jacobs was arrested. He wanted Abby to get in touch with her contact at the local police station. She did and was told that Jacobs was arrested for stealing a car and was being held without bail because he was a repeat offender. The contact also told her the judge denied bail even though Jacobs had come into some money and could have covered his own bond. The police suspected it as stolen funds since the man had no credible source of income. He told the police the money he had, came from a claim he had put in for his accident. The police were not convinced because he was hazy about his accident.

Jack visited Jacobs in the police lockup and was confronted by an angry man.

"Got nothing to talk to you about," Jacobs said.

"I want to talk to you about your accident," Jack said.

"What accident?"

"The one that you made a claim on. You know, the one that put you out of work for weeks."

"Talk to my lawyer about that," Jacobs said.

:Who is your lawyer?"

"Guy by the name of Thornton?" Jacobs said.

They were sitting at a table in a small enclosure and a guard leaned in and said, "Time's up."

"Jacobs is on his way to prison for stealing a car," Jack told Abby. "I think that's a dead end."

"Well, you still have two more people to interview," Abby said.

The next person Jack wanted to interview was a woman in her fifties by the name of Estelle Francis who lived in a section of town that was once upper crust but went downhill and was now in the midst of a revival. Francis lived in a two bedroom bungalow on a quiet street lined with trees that were doing their best to get rid of the sidewalk. The result was a sidewalk that rose and fell depending on how far the roots of the trees had progressed. He had called to tell her he was coming to see her and she was welcoming.

"I don't fully understand why you want to see me," she said, "but it don't matter. I like having guests."

"I'm glad to hear that," Jack said. "I want to talk about your insurance claim."

"My insurance claim?" she said.

"Yes. The one you put in for your accident," Jack said.

"Oh that," she said, "they paid that already. I hope they're not asking for the money back because I don't have it. I used that money to pay off the mortgage on this house."

"No, They're not asking for the money. But they want me to investigate the circumstances surrounding your accident."

"What are you, some kind of detective?"

"Yes. I'm a detective," Jack said.

"You mean like that guy on tv. What's his name? Columbo." She said.

"Something like that," Jack said, "but Columbo is a cop. I'm private."

"You don't say," she said, "so what do you want to know?"

"Mrs. Francis," Jack started and she stopped him.

"No Mrs. I'm not married," she said

"Okay, Miss Francis," she stopped him again.

"How about Estelle? That's my given name."

"Okay, Estelle," Jack said, "can you tell me what made you put in a claim for such a high amount? Were you injured badly in your accident?"

"Naw. I had a sprained foot but my cousin put me on to this lawyer who said he could get me a lot of money from an insurance company. They're loaded anyway."

"The lawyer's name is Thornton. Right?"

"How do you know that?" she said.

"And the lawyer sent you to a doctor by the name of Shepard."

"Wow," she said, "You're good."

"Estelle," Jack said, "you were, unknowingly, part of an insurance fraud perpetrated by Shepard and Thornton. Did you ever read the fine print on your claim?"

"I never read the claim. All I did was sign on the bottom and next thing I got a check for a large sum. And I used it to pay off my mortgage."

"Did you take off work?"

"A couple days," she said.

"For your information your claim was for a month loss of pay among other things."

"Oh my God," she said, "what's gonna happen now?"

"Nothing to you. I'm convinced you were used," Jack said.

Jack stood to leave. "Thank you for seeing me," he said.

"So, that lawyer and that doctor are in big trouble, huh," Estelle said.

"Yep," Jack said, "but don't you worry. They used you and look on the bright side. You got a house out of it."

"Are you married?" she asked.

"No," he replied smiling, "'bye Estelle."

CHAPTER 17

"Steven Jacobs is at large," Abby said.

"How did he get to be at large?" Jack said, "the last time I saw him he was locked up tight in a holding cell."

Jacobs was being transported from his cell to the courthouse when he pleaded with the driver to stop to let him go to the bathroom. He said he needed to pee really badly. The driver pulled into a restaurant parking lot, walked Steven into the restaurant and asked the manager to allow his prisoner to use the restroom. The manager said it was okay as long as the guard took responsibility. The guard agreed and walked Steven to the door where he removed the handcuffs and told Steven to go ahead.

The manager became upset when several diners complained about having a handcuffed prisoner in their midst. He told the guard to wait until they were outside before he put the cuffs back on the prisoner. This was an opportunity Jacobs could not pass up. As soon as they were outside he swung at the guard with all his strength and knocked him to the ground. Then he took the guard's gun and shot him dead. He then took the prison transport van and made his escape.

The Chief of Police held a press conference and gave all the details of the escape to the public, with a warning that the escapee was armed and considered very dangerous. He had killed a guard.

Abby was on site on the highway watching for speeders when a prison transport van passed her. She thought nothing of it since the van was travelling at normal speed. Then it hit her. Jacobs had escaped in a prison transport van. She called her dispatcher to get more info on the escape van and decided to follow it at a safe distance while dispatcher tracked down the info she wanted. The van she was following was the one the murderer had used. Abby called for reinforcements and sped up to get closer. The van driver saw her in his rear view mirror and stepped on the gas. Abby activated her lights and siren and the chase was on. She saw a cruiser on the opposite highway cross the grassy median and join her.

The driver of the van realized he could not outrun a highway patrol cruiser with its powerful engine so, he pulled over onto the shoulder jumped out of the van made a dash towards the woods. Abby realized if he got into the woods it would be impossible to find him because those woods went on for several miles. She had to stop him now but he was running faster than she could. She yelled at him to stop. He stopped but instead of raising his hands to give up he brought up a gun and tried to shoot it out with Abby and that was a grave mistake. Without even seeming to take aim Abby put a hole in his head. He was dead before he hit the ground. He got off a shot but it went wild and the bullet embedded itself in a tree on the opposite highway.

By this time the other officer had caught up. "I'll go get that bullet," he said, "you may need it to establish you fired in self-defense."

"Thanks, she said, "this guy killed the guard that was transporting him to court."

"Wasn't very bright to keep the transport van," the cop said, "he called attention to himself."

"Steven Jacobs is dead," Abby said.

"Don't tell me," Jack said, "he tried a shootout with you and lost."

"Exactly," she said.

"Wait a minute," Jack said, "that was a joke."

"Not to Jacobs," Abby said, "that's exactly how it happened. I chased him down the highway, he stopped the van and started for the woods, I chased him on foot, he stopped to shoot it out with me and lost."

"Abby," Jack said, "if you keep killing my witnesses I will have no one to give to the insurance companies."

"This one deserved to die. He killed one of our own while he was being transported to court. What makes it so heartrending, the guard he killed was due to retire in two weeks after forty years on the force. I would like to go where they have Jacobs and shoot him again."

"I have found Shepard is in trouble financially," Jack said.

"What? How can that be?" Abby said, "Shepard is one the richest men in this town."

"Used to be," Jack said, "he's paying dearly to stay out of prison."

"He's being blackmailed?"

"By a man who secured his files," Jack said.

Shepard's receptionist put a call through to him and when he answered, Senac said, "You forgot this month's payment."

"No, you scumbag," Shepard said, "I didn't forget. You've bled me enough you leech. There is no more money coming to you."

"Hold on a minute, Doc," Senac said, "You decided you'll be better off in jail?"

"Go to hell, Senac," Shepard said and ended the call.

Senac was a leech as far as Shepard was concerned. He was through letting him ruin his life and it was time for the worm to turn. He parked on Senac's street about four cars down from his apartment building and watched the entrance. After about an hour Senac came out, looked down the street and went to his car. Shepard started up and pulled out to follow Senac. He did not have a plan and didn't know why he was following the man but he knew he had to take action to get the leech off his back. Senac was sucking him dry and he had to do something. He stayed behind Senac's car and followed him to the entrance and soon they were racing South. Shepard had no idea where they were heading but he stayed with Senac.

He knew they would soon be coming up on a bridge and he would make his move then. Just before they got to the bridge Shepard sped up and turned his car into Senac's. The surprise hit caused Senac to lose control and his car ended up on the shoulder. He tried to steer back onto the highway but his car hit the barrier and started down a steep embankment picking up speed as it went. Shepard parked on the shoulder and watched as Senac's car hit a boulder flipped upside down and entered the water on its back. It didn't take long for the car to sink. Shepard saw the wheels disappear under the surface of the river but

Senac never emerged from the car. He waited for about a half hour until the bubbles from the car finally stopped. He was sure Senac was gone.

His next move was to find his files. That required breaking into Senac's apartment. It took him a long time because he was no B and E man but eventually he was able to get in. As soon as he entered he saw a desk in the corner of the living room. He pulled out the middle drawer and his files were there with some cash. He took the files and the cash and exited the apartment. He sat in his car for a moment savoring the freedom he felt from having that leech off his back. But his euphoria was short lived.

CHAPTER 18

Senac was angry that Shepard was refusing to pay. He had already squeezed a large sum out of him and he didn't need the hassle of chasing him for more so, he did what he always intended to do. He typed a letter to the DA and enclosed it with copies of the files in a large envelope which he addressed to the DA and took it to the Post Office.

At mid-morning on a Monday two men showed up at Doctor Shepard's office asking to see him.

"Do you have an appointment?" the receptionist asked.

"We don't need one," one of the men said as he showed his badge. The receptionist mouthed the words, "FBI."

She dialed a number and spoke into the phone, "Margie, you better come out here." she listened and then said, "just come, please."

Margie came out from the back office. "What's going on? Oh, sorry."

"These men are from the FBI. They want to see Doctor Shepard."

"Oh, I see," Margie said, "I'm sorry, Doctor Shepard is away at a conference in Atlanta. I don't expect him back until tomorrow."

"Very well, We'll come back in a couple days."

They left the receptionist and Margie staring at each other in silence. When Margie went back to her office she called Shepard.

"What is it, Margie?" Shepard said, "I'm in a meeting."

"Two men from the FBI came in to see you. I thought you might want to know."

"What did they want?" Shepard asked.

"I don't know. They didn't say," Margie said. "They said they will come back in a couple days."

"Okay," Shepard said, "thanks."

He did not go back to his meeting. He had to figure out what was going on. If the FBI were involved it meant trouble, He was sure Senac had made copies of the files and sent them to the police. That was the only thing that made sense. *Even in death that bastard is still bleeding me*

, he thought. *There is no way I'm going to prison.* He made his decision. He sent an email to Margie telling her to close down the practice and tell the FBI to go to hell. He was leaving the country.

Shepard took the next flight back to Washington, rented a car and sneaked into his home. He retrieved his passport and all the money in his safe, packed a suitcase and drove back to the airport. There, he booked a flight to Nassau, the Bahamas where he owned a vacation house. Nassau was to be a temporary stop until he could arrange to go to Venezuela because that country had no treaty arrangements with the US.

Margie was dumbfounded when she read the email. She gathered all the other employees and told them what Shepard's email had said. They were now out of work and needed to find employment elsewhere. The two FBI agents arrived to find the office in disarray. When they asked what was going on Margie handed them a copy of Shepard's email.

Margie told them she had no idea this was coming and she did not know Shepard's reason for closing down a thriving practice.

"Your boss was running an insurance fraud," one agent told her.

She sank into a chair when she heard that. She had no idea this was going on under her nose.

"Do you know where he would go?" she was asked.

"No," she said, "this is all news to me."

"Does he own property, a vacation home or any other property outside the US?"

"She thought for a while then said, "he owns a vacation home in Nassau. He goes there whenever he needs to relax."

The agents thanked her and left them the odious task of informing all Shepard's patients they were now on their own.

The FBI contacted the police in Nassau and asked them to collar Shepard and keep him locked up until they could get down there to get him

THE HAMMER OF JUSTICE

Jack and Abby were in Nassau for some time off. They were in need of some R and R they said, so, they rented the same bungalow they always did whenever they were in Nassau.

The Bahamian Police picked up Shepard as he was driving his rental jeep towards his house. He saw them following him so he sped up in an attempt to lose them but he was driving in an area they knew very well and he didn't. He came to a sharp turn which he couldn't negotiate and the jeep ran into the bushes. He jumped out and ran around to the back of the house that was there. He crashed through the door and came face to face with a lady who was sitting at a counter reading a magazine. He had a gun in his hand. She was surprised but recovered quickly.

"Who are you?" she said, "and why are you pointing a gun at me?"

"Never mind who I am," Shepard said, "and this gun makes you my hostage." Just then a loud speaker came alive.

"Doctor Shepard. Come out with your hands in the air."

"You're Doctor Shepard," the lady said, "I'm Abigail Saunders. My partner and I have been trying to bring you to justice and here you are."

"Small world," Shepard said, looking at the bedroom door. "Tell you partner to come out with his hands up or you're dead."

"He's not here," Abby said.

Shepard pushed the bedroom door open and quickly stepped away from it.

"I told you he is not here. If it matters, he went to get the ingredients for our breakfast."

The loud hailer once again erupted. "Doctor Shepard you cannot escape, Come out with your hands up."

Shepard went to a window and broke a pane. "I have a hostage," he shouted, "if I die so does she."

Jack pulled up to the house he was renting and was confronted by six Bahamian police cars. He parked and jumped out.

"What the hell's going on here?" he said to no one in particular.

"Stand back, Sir," a cop told him, "this is a hostage situation."

"That's my house," he said, "what hostage situation?"

"We've been asked by the American FBI to arrest one Doctor Joseph Shepard and he is in there with a woman hostage."

"Give me that," Jack said grabbing the hailer. "Abby, it's Jack. Be cool. What does Shepard want?"

"Is that your wife?" the cop asked. Jack did not answer.

"Who is in charge here?" he asked.

"I'll take you to him," the cop nearest to him said.

Jack spent a few minutes telling the officer who he and Abby were and why the FBI wanted Shepard.

CHAPTER 19

"I want you all to back off," Shepard shouted, "you too, Peregrin. I would rather die than go to prison and if I die so does your lady."

"Don't do anything rash," Jack shouted back, "we can work something out." He was also telling Abby not to put her life in any more danger than it was in already.

"Do you know this man?" the officer in charge said. "he seems to know you."

"Only in name," Jack said.

The officer put the hailer to his lips and said, "Doctor Shepard, let us know your demands."

"Don't rush me," came back.

After a few minutes Shepard spoke his demands. "I want you to make arrangements for me to go to Venezuela."

The officer looked at Jack, "How does he expect us to do that?"

"He picked Venezuela because there is no extradition treaty with the US," Jack said.

"Maybe so but we don't have the facility to send someone off to Venezuela. Surely he must know this."

"We need to coax him out of the house," Jack said. "Tell him we'll take him to the airport and find a plane to take him to Venezuela."

"We can't do that," the officer said.

"I know that," Jack said, "we have to get him out of the house. Do it."

After a long time Shepard shouted. "Okay. But any funny stuff and the woman is dead."

"Understood," the officer shouted back looking at Jack.

It was a long time before the door opened and Abby emerged with Shepard close behind her with his gun on her spine.

"Nobody moves," Jack said to all the cops.

Shepard surveyed the scene. He saw the cops, he saw Jack, he saw a path that ran down towards the beach and decided to chance it. He pushed Abby forward so hard she stumbled. Then he took off at full speed down the path. Jack made to follow him but one of the cops stopped him.

"He won't get anywhere," the man said, "that path leads to a high cliff with nothing but rocks down to the water. And it's very deep there."

Abby was up and dusting herself off. "I think Shepard knows he's finished," she said, "but he's deathly afraid of prison."

They all followed the path. Jack picked up Shepard's gun where he'd discarded it. He was standing at the edge of the cliff unsure of what to do next. Then he spread his arms and dove into the water. But he misjudged. He hit a ledge below head first and broke his neck. His lifeless body bounced off the ledge and into the water. It was about ten minutes later a police launch entered the lagoon and found his body floating facing down in the blue water.

Jack retrieved the bag of groceries from his rental car and went into the house to prepare a delayed breakfast.

"Well, big guy," Abby said, "your ancestors must be doing a dance wherever they dance."

"Not so," Jack said, "this case dragged on too long. My ancestors would have solved it in a fraction of the time by doing a war dance and then letting the tomahawks fly."

It didn't matter what Jack's ancestors would have done; the insurance companies that hired him were impressed with his work. He had succeeded in bringing several people to justice. They petitioned the courts to allow them to seize all of Shepard's remaining assets to recoup some of their losses. Jack saw no reason to inform them that there was at least one instance where the crooks turned on each other.

Jack and Abby stayed on in Nassau for two more days enjoying the beach and the nightlife including a couple hours in one of the casinos. They both went home with less money in their pockets but they enjoyed the excitement of it.

THE HAMMER OF JUSTICE

On his first day back to work a fashionably dressed woman came in his office and sat in one of the client chairs. Jack rose to greet her offering his hand which she did not take. He sat back down and waited for her.

"I'm Mrs. Summerall," she said, "Anita Summerall and I need to hire a detective. Probably you will do."

"Tell me why you need a detective and I will tell you if I'll do," Jack said.

She stared at him in silence until he said, "I charge rent for that chair you're occupying."

"There are things I must know before I hire you," she said.

"Fair enough," Jack said, "what things?"

"Have you killed a man in the line of duty?"

"Would I be required to, if I work for you?"

"Quite possible," she said.

"I cannot answer that question," Jack said, "because that decision will be mine to make and only mine. Mrs. Summerall, this is beginning to be a waste of my time so, I will say good day to you." He rose with the intention of showing her the door but she kept her seat.

"My husband is being blackmailed," she said, "he won't tell me who the blackmailer is but I noticed large sums of money being taken from our accounts. I need a detective find out who is blackmailing him."

"And you expect there might gunplay involved," Jack said.

"I do," she said, "because I believe he's involved with very dangerous people."

"If I take your case he would be the first person I will interview," Jack said, "would this be okay with you?"

"I would expect you to," Mrs. Summerall said.

That evening Jack arrived home before Abby so he mixed up a batch of margarita and had two glasses with salt on the rims waiting for her. She threw her arms around him in greeting and when she saw the glasses prepared and waiting she drew him in for a kiss.

"I like a man who reads his woman's mind," she said.

"And I like a woman who knows how to show her appreciation," Jack responded.

"I'll go remove my uniform," she said, "and slip into something sexy."

"And I will get out the margarita and get dinner started," he said.

The something sexy she slipped into caused a fire to start in him. He met her at the bottom of the stairs, picked her up and carried her to the sofa.

"I think dinner may have to wait," he said.

"You're talking too much," she said, wrapping her arms around his neck and pulling him down to her lips.

END

"

.

"

THE HAMMER OF JUSTICE

Milton Keynes UK
Ingram Content Group UK Ltd.
UKHW042239011124
450424UK00001BA/84